IN NOVEMBER

Voyager Books
Harcourt, Inc.
Orlando   Austin   New York
San Diego   London

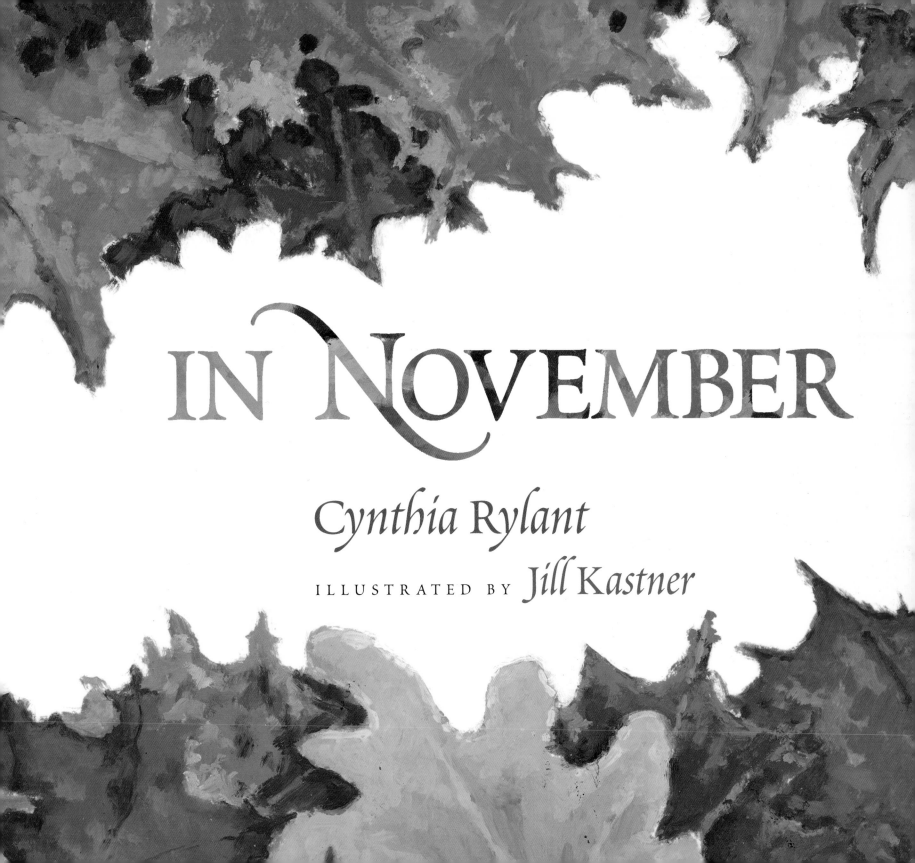

IN NOVEMBER

Cynthia Rylant

ILLUSTRATED BY Jill Kastner

For my mother
—C. R.

For Leah and Mack
—J. K.

In November, the earth is growing quiet. It is making its bed, a winter bed for flowers and small creatures. The bed is white and silent, and much life can hide beneath its blankets.

In November, the trees are standing all sticks and bones. Without their leaves, how lovely they are, spreading their arms like dancers. They know it is time to be still.

In November, some birds move away and some birds
stay. The air is full of good-byes and well-wishes.
The birds who are leaving look very serious. No silly
spring chirping now. They have long journeys and
must watch where they are going.

The staying birds are serious, too, for cold times lie ahead. Hard times. All berries will be treasures.

In November, animals sleep more. The air is chilly and they shiver.

Cats pile up in the corners
of barns.

Mice pile up under logs.
Bees pile up in deep, earthy holes.

And dogs lie before the fire.

In November, the smell of food
is different. It is an orange smell.
A squash and a pumpkin smell.
It tastes like cinnamon and can
fill up a house in the morning,
can pull everyone from bed in
a fog. Food is better in November
than any other time of the year.

In November, people are good
to each other. They carry pies
to each other's homes and
talk by crackling woodstoves,
sipping mellow cider.

They travel very far on a special November day just to share a meal with one another and to give thanks for their many blessings—for the food on their tables and the babies in their arms.

And then they travel
back home.

In November, at winter's gate, the stars are brittle. The
sun is a sometime friend. And the world has tucked her
children in, with a kiss on their heads, till spring.

www.HarcourtBooks.com

First Voyager Books edition 2008

Voyager Books is a trademark of Harcourt, Inc.,
registered in the United States and/or other jurisdictions.

The Library of Congress has cataloged the hardcover edition as follows:
Rylant, Cynthia.
In November/Cynthia Rylant; illustrated by Jill Kastner.
p.   cm.
Summary: Describes the autumn activities and traditions that
November's cooling temperatures bring.
[1. Autumn—Fiction.]   I. Kastner, Jill, ill.   II. Title.
PZ7.R982In   2000
[E]—dc21   98-22276
ISBN 978-0-15-201076-8
ISBN 978-0-15-206342-9 pb

C E G H F D B

The illustrations in this book were done in oil on paper.
The display type was set in Poetica.
The text type was set in Berling.
Color separations by SC Graphic Technology Pte Ltd, Singapore
Printed and bound by Tien Wah Press, Singapore
Production supervision by Christine Witnik
Designed by Lydia D'moch